Who am I?
r, The Modern Frankenstein

Emma Howell

Founder Editors: Bill Bowler and Sue Parminter

Illustrated by Jen Taylor

nma Howell lives in Oxford with her family, where she teaches Creative Writing. In her are time she enjoys reading, walking and going to the theatre. Emma loves nature and is ways looking out for birds, butterflies, and animals wherever she goes. As well as writing ays and books, Emma enjoys travelling and having adventures with her two sons.

OXFORD
UNIVERSITY PRESS

Great Clarendon Street, Oxford, OX2 6DP, United Kingdom

Oxford University Press is a department of the University of Oxford. It furthers the University's objective of excellence in research, scholarship, and education by publishing worldwide. Oxford is a registered trade mark of Oxford University Press in the UK and in certain other countries

First published in Dominoes 2016
2020 2019 2018 2017 2016
10 9 8 7 6 5 4 3 2 1

ISBN: 978 0 19 460922 7 Book
ISBN: 978 0 19 462242 4 Book and Audio Pack

Printed in China

This book is printed on paper from certified and well-managed sources

ACKNOWLEDGEMENTS

Cover image by: Getty Images (teenagers/Image Source)

Illustrations by: Jen Taylor

The publisher would like to thank the following for their permission to reproduce photographs: Alamy Stock Photo p.19 (school bus/robertharding).

Contents

ACTIVITIES

BEFORE READING

1 Here are some characters from *Who am I?* Match them with the sentences. Use a dictionary to help you.

1 Vic

2 Justine

3 Will

4 Henry

5 Elizabeth

6 Mr Waldman

a .... has long hair.
b .... is a teacher at the school.
c .... is tall and has brown eyes.
d .... has lots of friends and is nice to everyone.
e .... is very beautiful and likes to sing.
f .... is not happy and wants a friend.

2 *Who am I?* is a modern *Frankenstein* story. What do you think will happen? Tick the boxes.

a ☐ A boy starts a job and makes new friends.
b ☐ A boy is sad because he has no friends.
c ☐ A boy makes 'a monster'.
d ☐ Someone finds out who the monster really is.
e ☐ The police catch a criminal.

CHAPTER ONE

The boy who wants a friend

Every morning Vic waits for the school bus and he sees Justine. For two years they have taken the same bus every day. But Justine never speaks to him, never looks at him, never smiles at him. Every morning Vic thinks, 'Today, I'll talk to Justine. It's easy. I'll say "Hi", that's all I need to do.' But he stays quiet and does not speak. He is afraid she is going to laugh at him.

On the bus to school he sits behind Justine and thinks, 'Today school's going to be different. Today everything's going to change.' But it never changes.

Vic wants to be **popular**. He wants to be like Justine, who has lots of friends. He wants to be one of them – the group who go for coffee after school, who go to the cinema together. He is always **left out**.

popular when a person has a lot of friends

left out not in a group of friends

He wants Justine to **invite** him to her birthday party. Everybody is talking about the party, but he knows she will not invite him. He goes to the same school as Justine and her friends, and they sit in the same **classroom** every day, but they never **notice** him. He feels **invisible**.

Vic is worried that they laugh at him, too. He thinks they laugh at his clothes, they laugh at his name, they say he is different. They have **fun** – they sing, they laugh, they dance, and Vic watches and feels unhappy.

He wants a friend. He knows how to be a good friend and enjoy himself. He wants to sit and laugh with someone at lunch, or meet a friend at the weekend and see a film at the cinema.

He does not understand – why is Justine popular? What does she do? Is it because she is beautiful? Why don't they like him? He doesn't know what to do. He doesn't want to be different. He wants to be the same as them. All he wants is a friend – is that too much to ask?

The next morning he arrives at the **bus stop** in a new shirt. He has changed his hair, and he is wearing a different coat. Perhaps this will be the answer. He smiles at Justine and he thinks, 'Today's the day.' He stands next to her. 'Hi, Justine,' he says.

Justine looks at him. 'Hi,' she says.

'OK?' he asks her.

'Yes,' she says and looks at him with her blue eyes.

Vic knows his face is red; he feels hot, and his mouth is open but he cannot speak. She is waiting and he cannot think of a thing to say to her. He looks afraid and Justine sees. She smiles and walks away.

Afterwards, when they get off the bus, Vic feels angry that he is invisible again. Justine walks into school and forgets him. Why does she think she is better than him? He thinks about this all day and it makes him unhappy and angry. He walks home, a long, slow walk. He does not want to see Justine and her friends. He knows they are laughing about him.

invite to ask someone to come to a party

classroom a room inside a school

notice to see

invisible when you can't see somebody or something

fun something that you like doing

bus stop where you wait for a bus

afterwards later, after

At the bus stop the next Monday, he stands at the back. But when Justine arrives he turns his face – he does not want to look at her. 'Who's that?' he thinks, when he sees a tall, **good-looking** boy with an expensive coat.

'A new boy, perhaps?' Vic thinks. 'I need to talk to him. Perhaps today is lucky, and I'll find a friend at last.'

'Hi, I'm Vic,' he says and smiles.

'I'm Will,' the boy answers, and Vic notices how tall he is.

The bus arrives. Will sits next to Vic.

'It's my first day at this school,' Will tells Vic. 'My family moved here last week because my Dad has a new job. But I really wanted to stay in my old house, and all weekend I worried about today.'

Vic understands how Will feels and he tries to help him.

'School is OK if you're careful,' Vic says, 'I know where everything is and I can show you around.' In his head he thinks quickly, 'What can I do to make Will like me?' He notices Justine is also looking at Will so he speaks again. He does not want Will to see Justine yet.

'I love computers,' Vic says, 'and I read lots of detective books.'

'Great,' says Will in a friendly voice. 'I love books, too. And football. Do you play football?' he asks. 'I was in the **team** at my old school.'

'No, I don't play football,' says Vic quietly.

good-looking beautiful

team a group of people who play sports together against another group

'Do you run?' Will asks. 'I go running most days.'

'Well, I walk a lot,' Vic says. He tries to sound happy, but he's worried. Perhaps Will is going to notice that he does not like sports.

Soon the bus arrives at school and there is no more time to talk. Everyone looks at Will as they walk into school and Vic is pleased. In the classroom, Vic sits next to Will. He notices that Justine and her friends are watching him – they are all interested in the mystery new boy.

Crash! Mr Waldman comes into the classroom, shutting the door noisily. He calls their names and stops when he says 'Will'.

'Ah yes, Will, you've just arrived today. I hope people are friendly and they're showing you around,' Mr Waldman says.

'Yes **Sir**, they are, thank you,' replies Will, and he smiles at Vic. Vic smiles too. He is so pleased and happy to be friends with Will. They listen to Mr Waldman, who gives them a lot of work to do.

'Boring,' Vic says quietly, and Will agrees. At last, the lesson ends and the **class** go outside. Some of the boys from the

sir you say this when you talk to an important man

class the group of people you are with at school

football team are playing and Vic notices that Will is watching them. He tries to think of something interesting to say, but the ball comes near them and Will **kicks** it.

'Come and play with us if you want,' a boy calls to Will. So Will leaves Vic and runs to play football. Vic stands and watches, left out again.

When it is time to go inside, Will is laughing and talking to the other boys. He smiles at Vic and they walk in together. The afternoon goes slowly and Will looks out of the window at the sun on the football field.

It's four o'clock and the students escape outside. Vic is packing his bag when he notices that Justine is talking to Will. Justine is laughing. Vic sees Will turn and smile at him, before he walks away with Justine and her friends.

'Why didn't he come back for me?' Vic asks, but there is no one to answer. 'Justine has got lots of friends already. Why does she want Will, too?'

There is nothing Vic can do to change things, but he decides that he will try to win Will back.

kick to hit something with your feet

READING CHECK

Tick the correct sentences and correct the false sentences.

a ☐ Vic goes on the ~~train~~ to school. ......bus......
b ☐ Justine waits at the bus stop. ....
c ☐ Justine has green eyes. ....
d ☐ Vic likes sports. ....
e ☐ Will is new at school. ....
f ☐ Will plays tennis. ....

WORD WORK

1 Unscramble the words to match the pictures.

...popular...

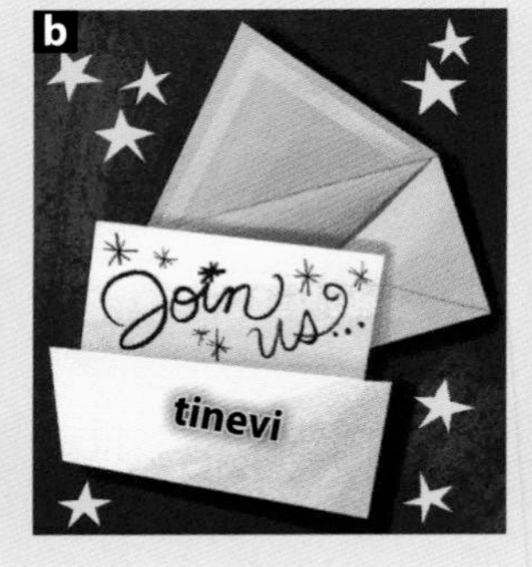

....

....

....

....

....

2 Use the words in the football to finish these sentences.

a Justine is very ...popular.... .

b Vic .... the new boy waiting for the bus.

c Will .... the football in the field.

d The group do not see Vic, he feels ....

GUESS WHAT

What happens next in the story? Tick three boxes.

a ☐ Vic plays football.

b ☐ Will and Justine go to the café.

c ☐ Justine asks Vic to go to the café.

d ☐ Will meets the group of friends.

e ☐ Vic feels sad and unhappy.

f ☐ Vic does something nice for Justine.

CHAPTER TWO
Alone again

Vic follows Will and Justine, but he is careful to hide so they do not see him. They walk slowly together to the café. Vic watches from outside as Will meets the other friends in the group. The girls talk to Will; they laugh with him and show him their phones. Some of the boys from the football team go into the café. They sit with Will too, telling **jokes** and stories about football games.

joke something that you say or do to make people laugh

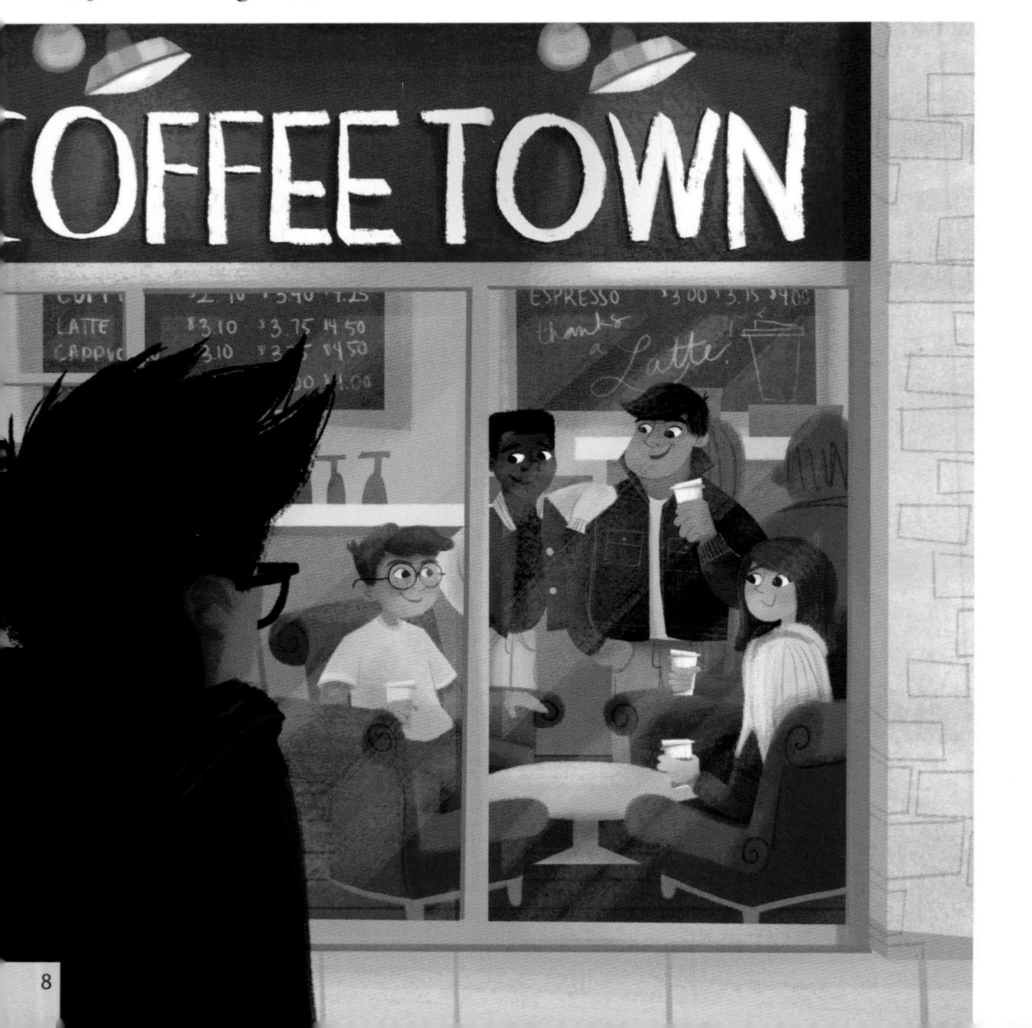

They buy coffees and colas, and then ask someone to turn on music. Vic sees they are enjoying themselves, but outside he is feeling cold as the sun hides behind the clouds. He walks to the café door. It looks warm inside and he has money to buy a drink. His hand touches the door, but he suddenly stops and thinks again. They did not ask him to come to the café, did they? They did not want him. He turns and walks away.

Why do they like Will? Why not him? Will has just arrived and suddenly he has got lots of friends. What is so good about Will? But Vic already knows the answer to his questions – Will is tall, good at football, and funny. The girls like him because he is good-looking with dark brown eyes, and he smiles at them. The boys like him because he is fast when he runs and he tells great jokes.

Vic feels unhappy; he feels **ugly**. He wanted to be in the café with them, not out on the road in the cold. It begins to rain and Vic's face is wet with rain and **tears** as he walks home.

'How was school today?' his mom asks brightly when he walks through the door.

'Fine,' he says crossly, turning his face away because there are tears in his eyes. 'Why does she ask the same question every day?' he thinks. 'It just makes me feel unhappy. I don't want to talk about things because nothing changes.'

Upstairs, he stays in his room. He begins to think hard.

'I know Mom loves me, and worries, but I don't want to tell her about Will and Justine. She wants me to be happy, I know that, but if she talks to people at school it'll be worse,' he says to himself.

'Dinner's ready!' Vic's mom calls. But Vic does not want to eat.

'I don't want dinner tonight, Mom,' he says. 'I feel ill. I think I need to sleep.'

His mom is worried, so she comes upstairs to look at Vic. His face is very white and he feels hot.

'OK,' she says. 'But call me if you need anything; perhaps a glass of milk?'

ugly not beautiful, bad to look at

tears the water that comes from your eyes when you cry

'Of course,' Vic says as he lies on his bed. 'Don't worry, I think I'm just tired.'

His mom touches his head and leaves him in the quiet bedroom. He listens while she goes downstairs and then he quickly turns on his computer.

Outside, it rains and rains and the wind hits the glass in the window. The sky is dark and heavy with rain. **Lightning**! Now, the sky is white with light and suddenly he knows the answer. He is invisible in the dark but when there is lightning he can see his face in the window. Now you see him and now you do not. And because they do not see him in the dark on his computer he can do what he wants.

lightning the light in the sky when there is a storm

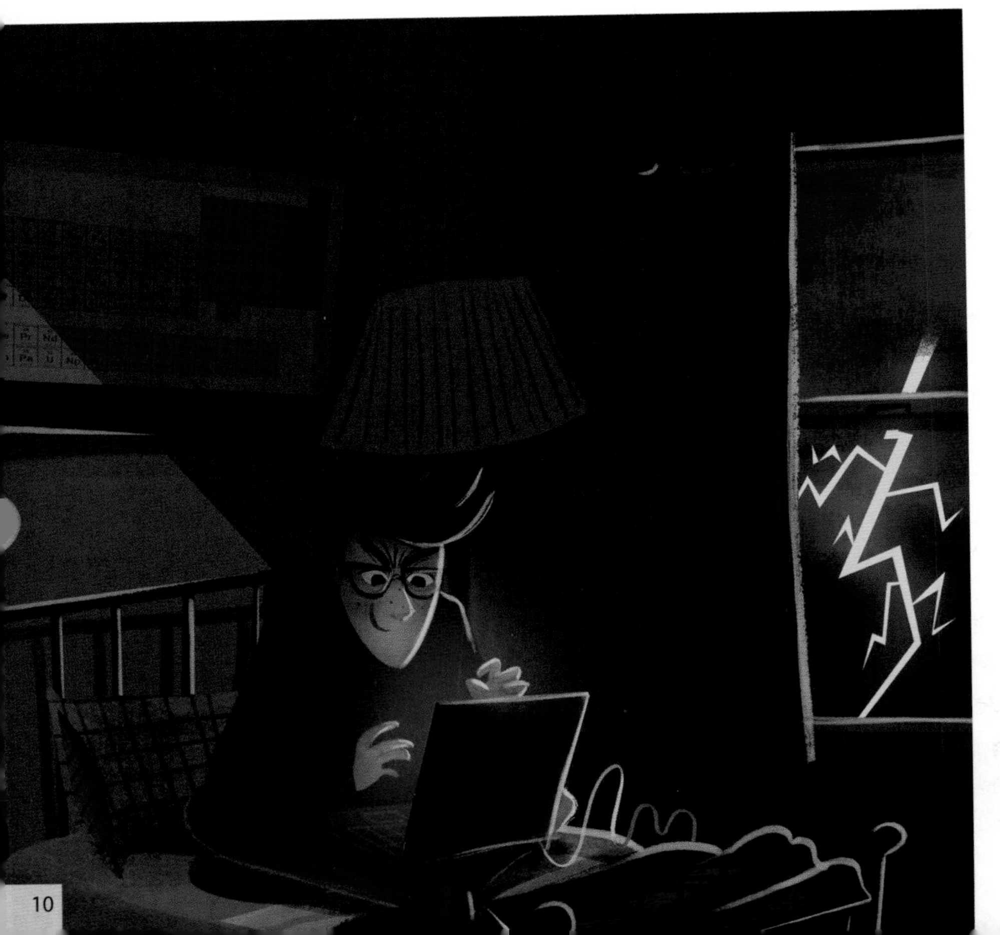

When he looks out of the window at the dark sky and the lightning, he knows he is right. He is going to make Justine and her friends listen. He will have **revenge**; he is going to make them so unhappy they forget who they are.

'Will, you liked me when we met, so if you're alone and afraid, perhaps you'll be my friend again,' he thinks. 'Perhaps you'll understand that I'm alone, too.'

Vic reads the newspapers and sees stories every day about people using their computers in clever ways. 'I can use my computer, too,' he thinks. 'For revenge.'

'I can listen to Justine and her group in the café, watch them at school, and photograph them when they walk home.'

'I need to become a detective to find out their secrets. First, I must find the **website** where they talk and then, make a new name for myself,' he thinks, and he feels excited. He is quick and clever when he works on the computer and soon he is looking at the website. There are lots of photographs of them having fun, dancing, going out and eating together, and **messages** they have sent. He reads them all.

'I must learn how to send messages and photographs next,' he thinks, and he writes down everything he needs to do.

'I can change what they say. I'll write bad things and make their photographs ugly. Everyone is going to know their secrets.'

'When they read the messages they'll be afraid, they'll think their friends don't like them. When they're **scared** and feel as invisible as me, I'll talk to them and do nice things. I'm going to be their new friend and, when that happens, the messages can stop,' Vic tells himself.

He thinks for a minute. Then, there's more lightning.

'Perhaps someone will find out I'm sending the messages,' he worries. 'I can say it was funny, a joke. Something to make people laugh and not to make them unhappy. No one needs to know the true **reason**. That's my secret.'

Tomorrow he will begin.

revenge when you do something bad to someone because they did something bad to you

website a place on the internet where you can find information about people or things

message you write this to someone and you send it with your computer or phone

scared afraid

reason why you do something

ACTIVITIES

READING CHECK

Match the first and second parts of these sentences.

- **a** Vic feels unhappy; — **3**
- **b** His mom is worried,
- **c** Outside it rains and rains
- **d** The girls talk to Will;
- **e** Will has just arrived
- **f** I need to become a detective
- **g** It is warm inside

1. they laugh with him and show him their phones.
2. and he has money to buy a drink.
3. he feels ugly.
4. and suddenly he has lots of friends.
5. to find out their secrets.
6. and the wind hits the glass in the window.
7. so she comes upstairs to look at Vic.

WORD WORK

Read the clues and complete the puzzle with new words from Chapter 2 in the correct form.

1▸ m e s s a g e s

1. Vic learns to send . messages . .
2. Will likes to tell . . . .
3. Everyone is going to be . . . .
4. Vic's face is wet with rain and . . . .
5. Vic can use his computer for . . . .
6. The place the friends use on the computer is called a . . . .
7. The . . . . why Vic writes the messages is he wants a friend.

Now read the blue squares in the puzzle to reveal the mystery word.

s _ _ _ _ _ _

GUESS WHAT

Guess what happens in the next chapter. Tick two pictures.

a ☐

b ☐

c ☐

d ☐

CHAPTER THREE

The plan begins

'Hi,' says Justine when she sees Will at the bus stop in the morning, and he smiles at her.

Will looks for Vic, who is standing at the back, and smiles. Vic thinks, 'The only reason he did that is to look like a nice person.' Then he tries to listen to Will and Justine talking.

'Hi Justine! Thanks for the message inviting me to your party, it sounds exciting,' Will says. 'Tell me about the people coming to the party so I know a little more about them.'

'Not me,' thinks Vic, 'Justine never invited me.' And he remembers the lightning and his revenge. Will and Justine sit together on the bus and talk about the different people. They do not notice that Vic is behind them, and he is listening to every word.

Justine begins, 'Elizabeth is coming. She was in the café – she was the girl with long, **blonde** hair. Her **parents** give her lots of presents. She's so lucky.'

Vic takes a photo of Justine and Will with the camera on his phone. He is careful. He does not want people to see him.

Justine **carries on** talking. 'I don't know if Henry can come,' she says. 'He was sitting next to Elizabeth in the café. He likes computers and is **awesome** at photography. Henry's everybody's friend. He can help with your **homework** because he understands everything. His parents visit different countries for their work so he speaks lots of different languages.'

Henry, Henry, Henry.

The name makes Vic angry. He does not like Henry because he is so nice to everyone. He even talks to Vic.

'I want someone who's *my* friend, not someone who's friends with everybody in the school,' Vic thinks.

Vic carefully writes down what Justine says. Then all through the morning lessons he watches and listens, taking photos with his phone. When it is time for lunch, Vic sits near the group of friends.

blonde yellow

parents mom, dad

carry on to go on doing something; to not stop doing something

awesome very good

homework when you learn at home, usually in the evening or at the weekend

Justine, Elizabeth, Will, and Henry are all laughing and joking. Vic listens and stays invisible, but he feels very alone watching the friends sitting happily together.

'Hey Justine, look at this,' says Elizabeth and she shows her friend a beautiful gold **locket** around her neck. 'It's a present from my mom,' she explains. 'It has a photo of her inside.' She smiles, but Vic thinks she is secretly **sad**.

Everybody looks at the locket – it is very expensive and the gold is bright in the sun. Vic takes a photo of the locket but he thinks it is ugly. Elizabeth is careful to hide the locket under her shirt. Henry looks at Elizabeth and asks if she is all right, because he knows her mom is ill in hospital.

'Is your mom any better?' asks Henry, but Elizabeth does not answer.

Henry then puts his hand on Elizabeth's arm and smiles, 'If you need my help you can ask me any time.'

Vic is standing very close and he takes a photo of Henry's hand on Elizabeth's arm. He starts to feel unhappy – he wants to help, he wants to ask Elizabeth if she's OK.

Suddenly, everybody in the group begins to talk about the party again. They are all so happy that Justine has invited them, and Justine is very excited too. She has a new blue dress and new shoes to wear, and her parents have said that the party can finish at midnight.

Will laughs. 'Do I need a new shirt?' he asks. Justine looks at Will with his big, brown eyes and Vic knows she likes him. Vic takes more photos.

'I can bring my guitar if you want. I'm awesome at playing the guitar,' Will laughs, and Vic walks away.

Vic thinks about his revenge and the gold locket comes into his head – that ugly, expensive locket. He remembers Henry and Elizabeth. He has a **plan**.

Vic hides behind the **lockers**, waiting and looking for Elizabeth. People come and go but they do not see Vic. Elizabeth

locket a little, flat, expensive box that you wear round your neck, usually with a picture of someone that you love in it

sad not happy

plan when you get something ready to do later; to get something ready to do later

locker a small cupboard with a lock, for keeping things in at school

and Justine arrive. Justine drinks a cola and talks to Elizabeth about Will.

'He's so funny, I like him a lot,' Justine says. 'But don't tell anyone, it's a secret. I don't want Will to know.'

Vic is bored, he does not want to hear how awesome Will is, he knows already. When is Elizabeth going to take off the locket? They are still talking and Vic is worried that his plan is not going to work. But then, Justine notices the clock and sees that she is late for tennis.

Vic watches Elizabeth take off the locket, put it in her bag, and put the bag inside her locker. Vic sees the number that opens and closes the locker door and remembers it. When Elizabeth goes outside, he opens the locker door and takes her locket.

He laughs. Elizabeth is going to think one of her friends took the locket, one of the friends she loves. Was it Henry, the boy who helps everyone? Was it beautiful Justine? Or was it the new boy, Will, with his big, brown eyes?

Vic hides the locket in his pocket and begins to walk home. He walks past Elizabeth and Justine playing tennis. He sees Will playing football and Henry sitting in the sun with his computer. They are all friends today, but what about tomorrow?

ACTIVITIES

READING CHECK

Correct the mistakes in the sentences.

a Vic is standing at the ~~front~~ of the bus stop. .....back.....
b Elizabeth has short, blonde hair. ....
c Henry likes computers and is awesome at sports. ....
d It is a beautiful, silver locket. ....
e Will puts his hand on Elizabeth's arm and smiles. ....
f Justine has a new red dress and new shoes to wear. ....
g Justine drinks a coffee and talks to Elizabeth. ....
h Vic walks past Justine and Elizabeth playing music. ....

WORD WORK

1 Match the words from Chapter 3 with the definitions.

a parents	**1** very good
b plan	**2** yellow colored hair
c homework	**3** work you must do for school when you are at home
d blonde	**4** to want to do something
e awesome	**5** mom and dad

2 Use the words from Activity 1 to complete the sentences.

a Elizabeth's ..parents... give her lots of presents.
b Elizabeth has long, ... hair.
c Will is .... at playing the guitar.
d Vic has to finish his .... in the evening.
e Vic has a .... to take the locket.

ACTIVITIES

GUESS WHAT

What happens in the next chapter? Tick a box to finish each sentence.

a When he gets home Vic…
  1 ☐ talks to his parents.
  2 ☐ writes messages for the website.

b The next morning Will…
  1 ☐ is waiting for Justine at the bus stop.
  2 ☐ talks to Vic at the bus stop.

c Justine is unhappy because the message on the website says that…
  1 ☐ Will is going to the cinema with a girl from his old school.
  2 ☐ Henry is going to the cinema with Elizabeth.

d Henry is sad that…
  1 ☐ Will is not talking to him.
  2 ☐ Elizabeth thinks he is not her friend.

CHAPTER FOUR

Who is #afriend?

At home, Vic goes to his room and sits at his computer. First, he must hide Elizabeth's locket underneath his desk – no one looks there. He gets his **notebook** out of his bag, and he looks at the photographs on his phone. He is pleased; the pictures are good, and he knows how to change them.

His mom calls him downstairs. She wants to talk to him.

'I'm sorry,' Vic says. 'I have so much work to finish for school. I can't talk tonight.'

He turns on the computer and goes to the website the friends use and he reads everything slowly and carefully. The messages Vic writes need to look like the other messages. He wants the friends to think one of them is writing the **nasty** messages and taking the photos.

notebook a small book where you write

nasty not nice

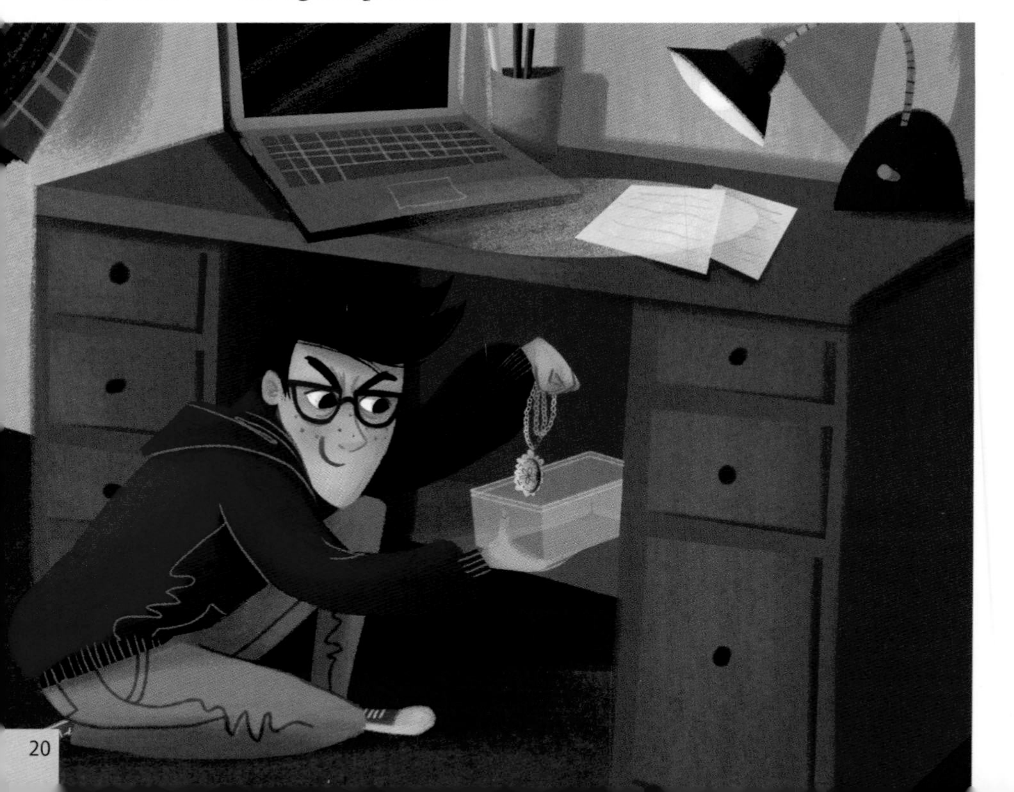

Now his dad calls him and says it is time for dinner. Vic sits at the table but stays quiet and does not eat much food. He is not interested in his parents and hurries back to his room. He closes the door loudly.

Oh, no! says his mom. 'What's wrong with Vic these days? Why is he always unhappy?'

His dad does not know. 'He's changing; he's older. Who knows, perhaps there's a girl he likes?' His dad says this because he does not want Vic's mom to be unhappy. They sit quietly but they don't know how to help Vic. Where's their happy boy? Who is this **stranger** who does not talk or eat with them?

Upstairs Vic is busy reading the notebook again and writing messages:

'Justine loves Will, but he thinks she's ugly.'

'Justine thinks she's beautiful, but she isn't.'

'Elizabeth says Henry makes her feel ill.'

'Will laughed at Justine playing tennis.'

'Henry writes everything you say on his computer.'

'Will is going to the cinema with a girl from his old school – he never liked Justine.'

Next, Vic looks at the photos. He changes the faces: he makes Justine look ugly, and he makes Will look boring. He writes next to the photo of the locket: *'Where is it? Who took it? It was one of your friends, Elizabeth...'*

He changes Henry's face in the photo, and changes Elizabeth's blonde hair – they do not look beautiful or happy now.

Vic touches his computer **screen** and sends the messages and photos. Now they are on the website for everybody to read. It says the messages are from '#afriend'. He smiles. Time to sleep; he will be busy again in the morning. Notebook, phone, and computer – everything he needs for revenge.

stranger someone you do not know

screen the glass on a computer or TV you look at

#afriend

log out

MENU

News

Messages

Friends

Games

Photos

#afriend shared a photo:

#afriend
Justine loves Will but he thinks she's ugly.

#afriend
Elizabeth says Henry makes her feel ill.

#afriend
Will is going to the cinema with a girl from his old school. He never liked Justine.

The next day Justine arrives late at the bus stop. Will is waiting for her. He is looking for her, and Vic wants to see what happens.

'Hi, how are you?' says Will, smiling. Justine does not smile. Her blue eyes are red with tears. Will looks at Justine. 'Are you ill? You look different.'

Justine sits quietly on the bus, but Will talks. When they get off the bus, Justine turns to Will. 'Is it true?' she asks him.

'Is what true?' Will asks. He does not know what Justine is talking about.

'You know,' Justine says angrily and she leaves.

Now Vic knows that Justine has seen the messages and photos. As they walk into school, Vic stays near Will and listens when he talks to Henry.

'I don't know what to do. I thought Justine liked me, but she's so different with me today,' Will says.

'I'm not surprised,' says Henry, and he hurries away.

Will follows Henry. 'What is it? Why are you being strange today?' he asks. Henry stays silent.

Will carries on talking. 'Justine asked, "Is it true?" but I don't know what she means. Do you know, Henry?' he asks. 'What's happening? Please tell me.'

Henry looks at him. 'Didn't you see the messages and the photos? Didn't you read what they said about you?'

Will shakes his head. 'What messages?' he asks.

'On the website,' says Henry. 'The message from #afriend. It says you don't like Justine and you're going to the cinema with a girl from your old school.'

'I don't know anything about that,' says Will. 'Nobody has told me about it.'

Suddenly Elizabeth comes in, crying. Henry goes to Elizabeth and touches her arm, but she moves away from him.

Elizabeth shakes her head. 'Stop it Henry,' she says. 'Did you take my locket? Or was it you, Will?'

Henry looks at Will and Elizabeth. 'How can you say that, Elizabeth? I'm your friend; I didn't take your locket.'

Vic hides behind the lockers with his notebook and camera; he is pleased. Next, Justine hurries into the room.

'Who's doing this?' Justine asks angrily. 'Who's #afriend? And why? Why is someone writing these things?'

'Someone **hates** us,' says Henry.

'And someone has my locket!' cries Elizabeth.

At lunch they are like strangers. They do not talk about Justine's party, they do not laugh and smile. But Vic is smiling. Vic feels awesome today because he is #afriend.

hate to not like

ACTIVITIES

READING CHECK

Put these events from Chapter 4 in the correct order. Number them 1–9.

a ☐ Vic's mom and dad talk about Vic.
b ☐ The friends eat their lunch quietly.
c ☐ Justine is quiet on the bus.
d ☐ Will talks to Henry.
e ☐ Vic goes home and sits in his room.
f ☐ Elizabeth tells Henry to leave her alone.
g ☐ Vic is busy reading and writing messages.
h ☐ Vic sends the messages to the website.
i ☐ Vic hides the locket under his desk.

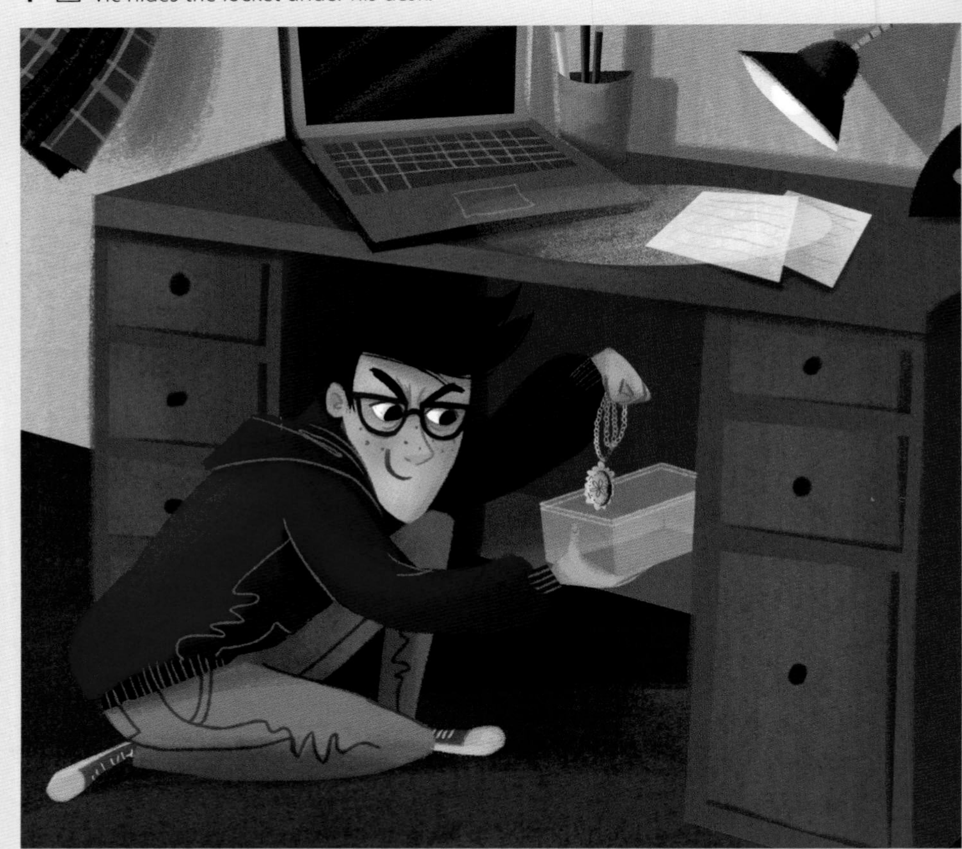

ACTIVITIES

WORD WORK

Use the words in the box to complete Vic's diary.

carry on	hate	nasty	notebook	sad	screen	~~stranger~~

Today at school, Will, Justine, and Henry were unhappy. Justine did not want to talk to Will. Will looked like a ..stranger.., he did not know what was happening. I have written what they said in my .... and I will change their words. When they see the .... messages on ...., they will be .... They will not .... being friends. Perhaps they will .... each other!

GUESS WHAT

What happens in the next chapter? Match the first and second parts of the sentences.

a Will puts his arm
b Mr Waldman tells the class
c Vic walks behind Justine
d Will asks Justine
e Vic feels tired;
f Vic's mom is pleased to see

1 Vic looking happy.
2 'you know I am not writing the messages?'
3 he wants someone to understand him.
4 a detective is coming to school.
5 and he can hear she is crying.
6 around Justine.

CHAPTER FIVE

Who is the monster?

That evening, Vic walks through the door of his house with a smile on his face.

'Hi Mom, I'm home. How are you?' Vic asks.

His mom is pleased to see Vic looking happy again. She smiles at him and gives him a drink and a **snack** to eat. 'How was school today?' she asks Vic.

'Today was a very good day, it was awesome,' he says. 'I think school is going to be much more fun now. I really like the new work I'm doing on my computer.'

His mom asks more questions about school, but Vic says he needs to finish his homework. He then hurries upstairs to his room. His dad phones later and asks if Vic is better.

'Oh yes,' his mom says. 'He's happy; he said today was awesome. It's wonderful to see him smile.'

'Good,' replies Vic's dad, 'I'm very pleased. I'm going to be late home tonight because work's very busy. But it's good to hear that Vic's happy. I began to think he was ill or there was a **problem** at school.'

The next morning, Vic walks behind Justine to the bus stop and he can hear she is crying. She has changed. Usually, she sings when she walks to the bus stop, or sometimes she dances, but not today. Vic's plan is working, she is unhappy and very soon she is going to want to be friends with him.

'Hi Justine, are you OK?' he asks.

He knows his plan will work and Justine will want a friend like him.

'I'm OK. I've got a **headache**, that's all,' she replies. She moves away from Vic and looks for Will.

'Can I help you?' Vic asks.

'No. Stay away from me,' she says angrily, 'I don't want your help.'

snack something small you eat that is not a meal

problem something that makes you feel bad; something difficult

headache a pain in your head

'Justine, are you all right?' Will shouts and he runs quickly to the bus stop. Will is very tall. Vic feels small and ugly when Will looks down at him.

'What are you doing?' he asks.

'Nothing,' replies Vic, 'I wanted to know if she was OK.'

'Leave me alone,' Justine says to Vic, 'I don't want to talk to you.'

'Sorry,' Vic says quietly. People at the bus stop are watching him and he wants to hide.

Vic moves away from Justine. He watches unhappily as Justine moves nearer to Will and she puts her head on his arm. Will puts his arm round Justine and they walk onto the bus.

'I'm happy to see you,' Justine says to Will. Will smiles at Justine, his arm still round her. 'When we talked on the phone last night I knew I wanted to be with you.'

'And you know I'm not the person who's writing the messages?' Will asks Justine.

'Yes,' she says.

Vic listens carefully and does not understand. In his plan Justine hates Will – is his plan going wrong?

He feels cold and alone again. He needs to think of something. He puts his hand in his pocket and touches Elizabeth's locket. He knows what to do.

Vic waits at the door as they all walk into the classroom. When Justine comes near, he suddenly drops his books and homework. Will and Justine stop, and they help him to **pick up** his homework. He then quickly hides Elizabeth's locket in Justine's coat pocket.

'Thank you,' he says and smiles, knowing that soon everybody is going to hate Justine.

Their teacher, Mr Waldman, shouts at the class to be quiet.

'I have something important to say to one of you,' he says. 'There's a student in this class who's making people very unhappy. I don't know if you're planning this, but it needs to stop. Listen to me – I don't know who you are but I'll find you.'

The class quietly listen to their teacher. Henry shakes his head and looks at Elizabeth. Justine touches Will's hand.

Mr Waldman carries on talking, 'Someone has taken a gold locket from Elizabeth – an expensive locket. Elizabeth's parents are going to talk to the police and a detective is coming to the school. Worse still, this **monster** is writing nasty messages – messages which aren't true – and putting them on a website.

'This monster can't hide and very soon we're going to find out his or her name.'

All the class are quiet. Is it true? Somebody they know is doing these terrible things? Mr Waldman leaves the class and everyone starts talking.

pick up to take something in your hand

monster a person who does very bad things

'I think somebody has sold the locket – they wanted the money.'

'No, someone did it to make Elizabeth unhappy.'

'Have you read the messages?'

'I don't use the website, so I'm OK.'

'My mom wants me to change school.'

'I know, my dad says I mustn't walk home alone.'

Vic looks at their faces and feels tired; he wants someone to understand him. This was not the plan. He is not a monster. He wants a friend and that's the only reason for writing the messages. Now everybody is worried, and he is more alone. He suddenly wants it all to end. 'But it'll be OK,' he thinks. 'The police will come to the school, they'll find the locket, and they'll think that Justine is the monster.'

ACTIVITIES

READING CHECK

What do they say?

1 Hi Mom, I'm home.

2 ~~I'm OK, I've got a headache.~~

3 He's like our little boy again.

4 I'm happy to see you.

5 I don't know who you are but I'll find you.

6 I'm going to be late home tonight.

7 Justine, are you alright?

8 What are you doing?

a Justine says to Vic: I'm OK, I have a headache.

b Vic's dad says to Vic's mom: ....

c Will says to Vic: ....

d Vic says to his mom: ....

e Mr Waldman says to the class: ....

f Justine says to Will: ....

g Vic's mom says to Vic's dad: ....

h Will says to Justine: ....

WORD WORK

1 Match the words to the images.

a ~~monster~~
b headache
c pick up
d snack

1 ....

2 ....

3 ....

4 monster

2 Use the words in the computer screen to complete the summary of Chapter 5.

carry on, locket, snack, class, afterwards, fun, monster, headache, plan, classroom, fun

After school Vic eats a . . . . snack . . . . and then starts work on his computer. Vic's mom asks how school was today and Vic says it was . . . . The next day Justine looks unhappy and tells Vic she has a . . . . Vic talks to her but she tells him to go away and Will puts his arm around her. At the . . . ., Vic puts the . . . . in Justin's coat. . . . ., Mr Waldman tells the . . . . there is a . . . . who is putting bad messages on the website. Vic feels bad. This is not . . . . But he will . . . . with his . . . .

GUESS WHAT

What happens in the next chapter? Tick the boxes.

a ☐ Vic asks Henry for help.
b ☐ Vic asks Will for help.
c ☐ Justine and Will sit together on the bus.
d ☐ Mr Waldman asks to look in Will's bag.
e ☐ Mr Waldman asks to look in Justine's bag.
f ☐ Mr Waldman finds Elizabeth's locket.
g ☐ Vic finds Elizabeth's locket.
h ☐ Mr Waldman says the name of the monster.

CHAPTER SIX
The monster is found!

After school, Vic looks for Henry because he needs help with his plan and he is sure Henry is the right person to ask. He finds Henry outside. He's eating a snack at a table behind the school, with a computer beside him.

As Vic walks near to Henry he notices that he looks sad and worried. For a minute, Vic feels bad about Henry, but he quickly forgets. He tells himself, 'I can't be sorry for other people now, I need my plan to work so all this trouble ends.'

'Hi Henry,' Vic says, sitting down at the table.

'Oh hi,' replies Henry, who is surprised to see Vic.

'Henry,' Vic asks, 'Can you help me with a phone problem?'

'I can try, but I know more about computers than phones. What's the problem?' Henry asks.

'Do all phones use the same **memory card**?' Vic asks.

'Some do,' Henry says. 'But why do you want to know that? Your phone has a memory card in it already – you don't need two memory cards.'

Vic thinks quickly, 'Something has happened to my phone and it isn't working. When I take a photograph nothing happens. I'm sure all I need is a new memory card, that's all, and I want to buy the right one.'

'Memory cards are expensive, but you can find a cheap one on the internet if you're lucky,' Henry tells him. 'Why don't you take it back to the shop? They know all about phones, and it's easy for them to see which memory card you need.'

Vic's face is turning red. 'Oh, it was a present. I'm not sure where my mom bought it and I don't want to tell her it isn't working.'

'Oh,' says Henry, 'OK.'

Vic wants to leave because Henry is asking a lot of difficult questions now.

'OK, thanks for your help. See you tomorrow,' says Vic, walking away. But Henry is quiet and he looks worried again.

Back in his room, Vic starts work at once. He finds the photo of Elizabeth's locket and writes a message under the picture:

Justine always takes what she wants.

Next, he finds the photos of Will, Justine, Elizabeth, and Henry. If he does everything right, he can change the pictures on his computer. It is boring and it takes a long time but, in the end, he finishes his work and he is pleased. The pictures are awesome – no one can see the changes he has made. The photos are of Henry with his hand on Justine's arm and another of Henry with his arm around Justine.

memory card a small, flat square inside a phone which has all the photos in it

'When Will and Elizabeth see these pictures they're going to be unhappy – Justine and Henry together in secret. If they think the photographs are real, then they'll also think it's true that Justine is the monster,' Vic says to himself.

His work is nearly finished and now he needs a snack before he goes to sleep. He is going to be very busy tomorrow. He has a headache because his eyes are tired from looking at the computer screen all night.

He goes downstairs and says 'goodnight' to his parents. He needs everything to look the same as usual; his parents must not notice anything different or his plan will not work.

The minute it is **daytime**, Vic starts his computer. It is time for the end of his plan. He touches the screen and sends the message to the website. Now everyone can see the picture of the locket and the photos of the friends.

Next, he takes the memory card out of his phone and puts it in his pocket. Everything is ready; he knows what to do. He shouts goodbye to his mom and runs to the bus stop – he does not want to be late today.

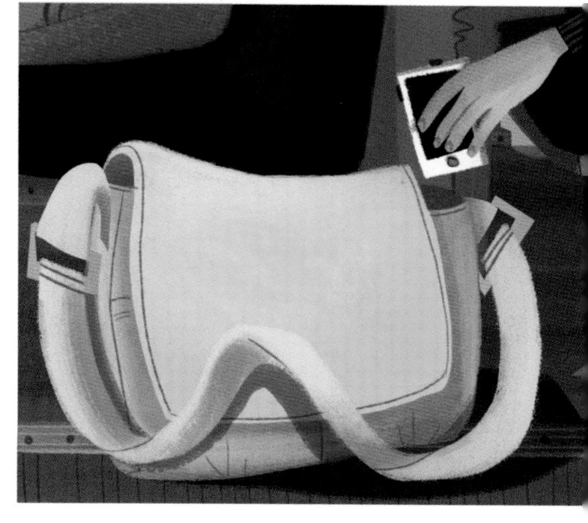

Justine and Will are together again, but he is not worried. Soon everything will change. They do not look at Vic as they sit on the bus, talking quietly. 'Good,' thinks Vic, 'they're busy **chatting** and they won't notice what I'm doing.'

He moves nearer to the seat in front. He looks around – no one can see him, he is sure. Slowly and carefully he puts his hand in Justine's bag and takes her phone. He pushes open the back of the phone and quickly changes the memory card with the one in his pocket. Now all the photos that he took are on Justine's phone.

He hides the phone back in Justine's bag and sits in his seat, looking out of the window. When the bus stops at school he stays for a minute and gets off after Will and Justine. He looks behind him; he feels worried. Did anyone see him change the memory card? No, he is sure they did not.

When Vic walks into the classroom, everybody is chatting excitedly. Elizabeth and Henry are looking angrily at Justine. Mr Waldman is waiting for Justine to sit in her chair. Everyone has turned to Justine and she feels scared.

daytime the time when it is day and not night

chat to talk to a friend

Is there a new message? What has happened now? Justine does not know. She has not looked at the website today because her parents said she must not use it again.

'Quiet!' Mr Waldman shouts to the class. 'I want everyone to listen very carefully. I'm going to ask some important questions and you need to think before you answer.'

Everyone feels scared and worried now. What is Mr Waldman going to say?

'Yesterday, I explained that Elizabeth's locket was **missing** and that someone, a monster, was putting nasty messages and photos on a website,' he said. 'Today, these terrible things are going to end. This morning, there are more photos and messages and they say the name of the person who took the locket. It's Justine.'

Justine's face is white. She cannot speak.

'Justine, I want to see in your pockets and look at your phone please,' says Mr Waldman.

Justine carries her coat and bag to Mr Waldman. She gives him her coat and she waits. She does not know how this is happening to her. Mr Waldman puts his hand in her pocket and he finds the gold locket.

Justine screams, 'No! I didn't take the locket! Please, Mr Waldman. It wasn't me, it's not true!'

Mr Waldman says nothing but he takes Justine's phone and touches the screen – all the photos and messages from '#afriend' are on the screen. All those terrible pictures and words are there, on Justine's phone.

'I've found the monster,' he says slowly. 'Justine, how could you do these terrible things to your friends?'

'I haven't done anything, someone is making it look like me,' Justine says. 'I never did any of this. Elizabeth, please! I have no reason to hurt you, Elizabeth.' She turns and looks at Will. 'Will, you know it's not true,' she cries.

Vic looks at the class. Elizabeth is crying and Henry is shaking

missing not in the usual place; not there

his head. Only Will is looking at Justine. He looks sad and worried. He wants to help her but he does not know what he can do.

Vic cannot look any more. He hears Justine scream, he hears Elizabeth crying. He wants to feel pleased that his plan has worked, but he does not feel great. He feels terrible. He starts to feel scared about what he has done.

READING CHECK

Are these sentences true or false? Tick the boxes.

		True	False
a	Vic asks Henry for help with a computer problem.	☐	☑
b	Henry looks happy and is eating a snack.	☐	☐
c	Henry says memory cards are expensive.	☐	☐
d	Vic says his dad gave him the phone.	☐	☐
e	Vic writes a message about Elizabeth's locket.	☐	☐
f	Justine and Elizabeth sit together on the bus.	☐	☐
g	Vic changes the memory card in Justine's phone.	☐	☐
h	Elizabeth's locket is in Justine's pocket.	☐	☐
i	Vic is happy about what happens.	☐	☐

WORD WORK

Use the words in the notebook to complete the sentences.

a School is in the ...daytime... .

b Vic wants to take the .... out of Justine's phone.

c Vic tells Henry he has a .... with his phone.

d Everyone in the class is .... excitedly.

e Elizabeth's locket is ....

GUESS WHAT

What do you think happens in the next chapter? Tick a box to finish each sentence.

a Henry...
  - **1** ☐ is angry with Justine.
  - **2** ☐ talks to Vic.
  - **3** ☐ tries to help Justine.

b Elizabeth...
  - **1** ☐ tells the police Justine took her locket.
  - **2** ☐ tells Mr Waldman Justine did not take her locket.
  - **3** ☐ tells the police Will sent the messages.

c Vic...
  - **1** ☐ has to go and answer questions about the messages.
  - **2** ☐ tells Mr Waldman he saw Justine take the locket.
  - **3** ☐ talks to Henry about the monster.

CHAPTER SEVEN

The detective

After Mr Waldman says that Justine is the monster, he takes her to the school office to talk to the police and the **head teacher**. Will stands up – is he going to speak? Vic watches but Will stays quiet and does not follow Justine. Vic sees tears in his eyes as he sits back down.

Everyone in the class is surprised that Justine took the locket. Some of the girls are quietly chatting:

'Justine is a criminal! Perhaps she stole other things!'

'I lost my watch – do you think Justine took it?'

'Is it true? Justine took her best friend's gold locket?'

'Do you think the police are asking questions already?'

'Her parents are going to be so angry with her.'

*'Perhaps she'll run and the police will **chase** her!'*

head teacher the most important person in a school

chase to run after someone or something

'Stop talking about Justine!' Vic wants to scream at them.

Vic feels he is in danger and there is one idea that he cannot get out of his head. 'Perhaps the monster that I've made is after *me*,' he starts to think. 'Perhaps it's chasing *me*.' But then he quickly says to himself, 'Stop being stupid. The monster isn't alive, it's only on the website.'

Just then, he notices Elizabeth talking quietly to Henry.

'We've been friends for years,' says Elizabeth. 'She stays at my house, talks to my parents.'

'I know,' Henry replies.

'How can Justine be a criminal? I know her. We do everything together,' Elizabeth says.

'I think something strange is happening,' Henry answers. 'Look at the photos this morning; they weren't true, so perhaps Justine isn't the monster.'

'And Justine knows my mom is in hospital. She knows how important the locket is to me, not because it's expensive but because of the photograph of my mom,' says Elizabeth.

Vic watches Henry with Elizabeth; he sees love in Henry's eyes when he looks at Elizabeth. Elizabeth looks so sad and worried about Justine. Vic does not understand – why is Elizabeth thinking about Justine, the girl who took her locket?

'Think, Elizabeth,' Henry says. 'We're always with Justine, aren't we? But we never saw her taking any photographs.'

'And did you notice Justine using her phone camera when we were in the café?' he **continues**. 'Did she take a picture of the locket? It's important we remember everything that happened.'

'She didn't,' replies Elizabeth, 'and Justine was playing tennis with me when the locket went missing from my locker. I didn't leave Justine alone at my locker, so when did she take it?'

'A detective can look at your locker, Elizabeth. The criminal touched your locker,' Henry says, feeling excited. 'They can look at people's fingers to find out who the true monster is in this class.'

continue
to start again after stopping

Vic never **imagined** Henry as a detective and he is worried. He knows how clever and quick Henry is - and now Henry is trying to **work out** the mystery to help Justine and Elizabeth.

'All these problems started when Will arrived,' Henry says to Elizabeth.

'Do you think it's Will, then?' asks Elizabeth and she sounds surprised.

'No, but I think it's something to do with Will...' Henry replies.

Vic turns away and sits quietly. He begins to feel worse and worse. All the things he has done, and he is still alone and scared without any friends to talk to.

In his plan, Elizabeth forgets Justine is her friend. Why are they still worried about each other? He starts to see that being a friend is not always easy. Henry carried on loving Elizabeth when she was angry with him. Will carried on liking Justine after Mr Waldman said she was the monster. Now Elizabeth and Henry are trying to help Justine.

imagine
to think of something happening in your head

work out
to find the answer to something

Suddenly Vic understands. This is why he did not have a friend – to have a good friend, first you need to *be* a good friend, even when things are difficult. He thinks, 'It is not too late for me to be a friend to Justine. I can think of something.'

Too late. Elizabeth stands up. 'I need to talk to the head teacher,' she says. 'I don't want the police to take Justine. I've got my locket back and I know Justine didn't take it, she's my best friend. I'll speak to my parents so they understand. There's something wrong and I want to find out what happened.'

Henry stands up, too. 'I'll come with you,' he says. 'I need to talk to the police about something that happened yesterday. I was worried about it last night, but now I understand. I think I have the answer and can help Justine.'

Henry and Elizabeth leave the class and Vic begins to get a headache. 'What is Henry the detective going to say to the head teacher and the police? What does he know?' Vic tries hard to remember everything he said to Henry yesterday afternoon.

Now the class are excited; suddenly everyone is chatting. They all want to know what Henry and Elizabeth are doing. Will starts to look better; he wants Justine to be back with him. He stands by the door, trying to see what is happening. Vic can hear him quietly saying, 'I know she didn't take the locket, I know she didn't take the locket.'

Many minutes later, Will suddenly says 'shh!' to the others in the class. 'There's another man going into the office. I think I know him, but where from?'

The next minute, the head teacher walks into the room with Mr Waldman. 'Sit down and be quiet!' their teacher says angrily.

Mr Waldman explains something quietly to the head teacher. Both of them look at Vic and the head teacher says slowly, 'You're Vic, aren't you?'

Vic quietly answers, 'Yes, sir'. He imagines the monster waiting for him. 'That's the trouble with monsters,' he thinks. 'You can't **control** what they do.'

'Come with me', says the head teacher. 'We have some questions to ask you. I'm trying to work out what's happened. I think people are wrong about the **identity** of the monster.'

He turns and speaks to the class. 'Control yourselves please, and wait quietly. Another teacher is arriving for your lesson and the police want to talk to some of you. Please answer any questions carefully; it's important we learn the true story.'

Vic walks slowly with the head teacher to his office. He begins to feel **faint**. As they turn the corner he sees Justine and Henry behind another door talking to the police. The head teacher opens the door to his office.

As Vic walks in he sees his parents waiting for him. Why are his parents here? Everything is going wrong. He suddenly understands that he cannot control anything that happens now.

His mom looks terrible, her face is very white and his dad is sitting and shaking his head. His dad has Vic's computer in his hands and on the seat next to him is Vic's notebook.

control to make people or things do what you want

identity who a person is

faint to fall down suddenly because you are afraid or ill; to feel like this will happen

ACTIVITIES

READING CHECK

Choose the correct words to complete the sentences about Chapter 7.

a Mr Waldman says *Justine* / *Elizabeth* is the monster.
b 'Is it true? Justine took her best friend's gold *locket* / *locker* ?'
c 'We've been friends for *months* / *years*,' says Elizabeth.
d 'Justine knows my *mom* / *dad* is ill in hospital.'
e Elizabeth starts to *laugh* / *cry*.
f 'A *teacher* / *detective* can look at your locker, Elizabeth.'
g 'I *do* / *don't* want the police to take Justine.'
h The class are *excited* / *angry*; suddenly everyone is chatting.
i 'There's another *woman* / *man* going into the office.'
j 'I think people are *right* / *wrong* about the identity of the monster. '

WORD WORK

1 Find five more new words from Chapter 7 in the word square.

H	E	A	D	T	E	A	C	H	E	R	T
R	U	L	B	C	A	N	O	A	P	U	Y
Q	X	O	P	W	B	O	N	V	R	O	I
F	O	A	K	M	J	T	T	N	A	L	W
A	W	E	Q	Z	X	H	R	K	D	C	F
I	M	A	G	I	N	E	O	E	X	S	A
N	C	H	A	S	E	E	L	I	N	B	K
T	P	L	R	I	D	E	N	T	I	T	Y

2 Use words from Activity 1 to complete the definitions.

a The .head teacher. is the most important person in the school.
b When you .... someone, you run after them.
c ....: when you think of something in your head.
d You tell someone what to do when you are in ....
e Your .... is who you are.
f People fall to the ground when they feel ....

GUESS WHAT

What happens in the last chapter? Write *Yes* or *No*.

a A detective talks to Vic. ....
b The head teacher tells Vic he knows he is the monster. ....
c Vic says Henry sent the messages. ....
d Vic says he sent the messages. ....
e The police take Vic away. ....
f The police take Justine away. ....
g Vic is sorry for what he has done. ....
h The head teacher says Vic must find a new school. ....

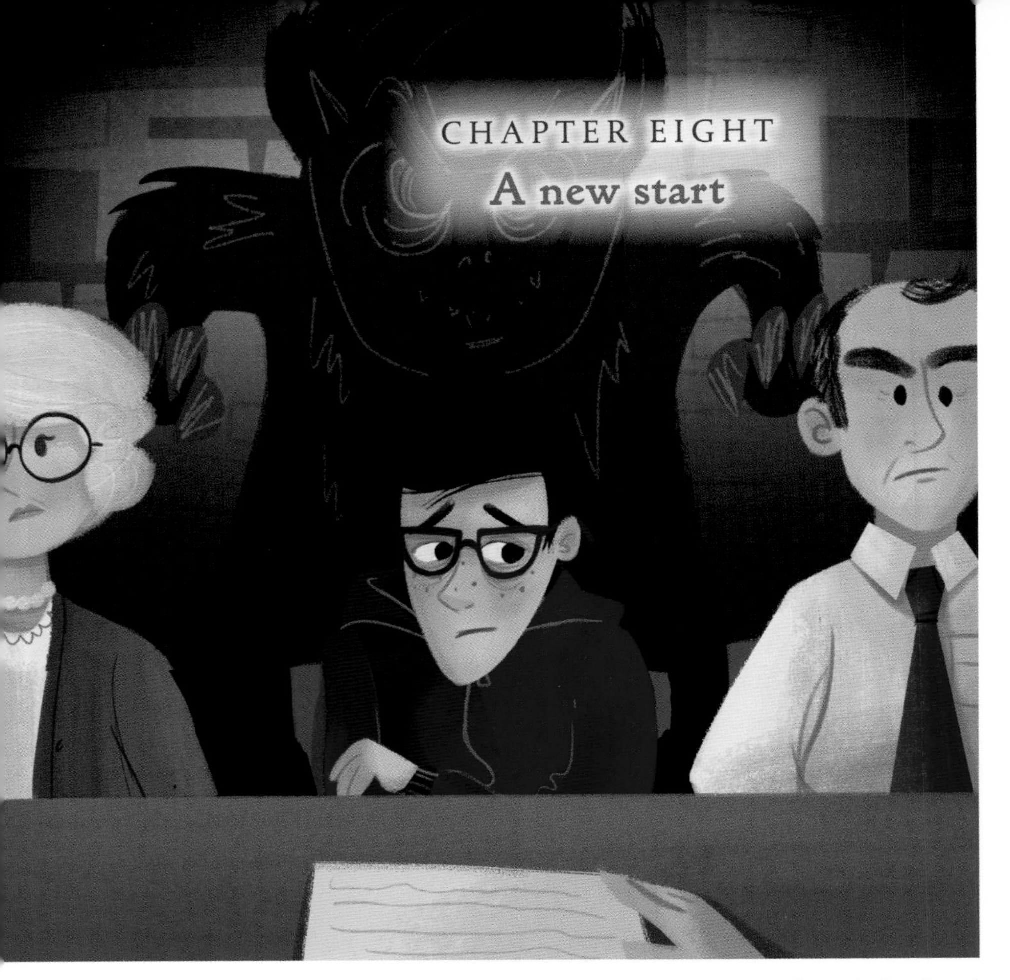

CHAPTER EIGHT
A new start

'I see you're surprised that your parents are here,' the head teacher says to Vic.

Vic **nods** his head, staying silent, as he cannot find the right words to say.

'I phoned your parents because I didn't want you to be alone at this difficult time,' the head teacher continues.

Vic nods again. He imagines the monster walking nearer to him and there is nowhere for him to escape. He is **trapped**.

The head teacher speaks quietly, 'Now Vic, it's time to tell us the **truth**. What have you done?'

'I've done nothing, sir. It's Justine, you saw her phone...' says Vic, too scared to say the truth.

nod to move your head up and down to say 'yes'

trapped when you can't get away from something

truth what is true

His mom looks at him, crying. 'Vic, I love you and I'm trying to understand what has happened,' she says. 'You need to talk to us so we can help you.'

Vic is thinking quickly, what can he do?

He is trapped by his monster. If he continues to lie everything will get worse.

'Vic, my son, talk to us,' his dad **whispers**, nodding at Vic to make him do the right thing.

He remembers Justine looking so scared; the faces of Will, Henry and Elizabeth. He thinks about how they carried on being friends. **Finally**, he looks at his mom again and sees how sad her face is. The time has come to tell the truth.

Before he can say a word, the head teacher says, 'You need to talk to us because we know you wrote the messages. We know you took the locket and we know you changed the memory card in Justine's phone. You have a secret identity: you are #afriend.'

Vic is surprised. How do they know the truth?

'It's true, isn't it Vic?' the head teacher continues. 'You are #afriend – the monster.'

Vic nods.

'Oh my boy, what have you done?' his mom says in a whisper.

'Henry talked to the police. He remembered that you chatted about trying to find another memory card and he thought that was strange. So when he saw the photos on Justine's phone today he quickly understood,' the head teacher says. 'It was your memory card in her phone.'

Vic's face turns white as he listens. It is a terrible thing he has done.

'Henry and Elizabeth noticed other strange things so they knew we were wrong about the identity of the monster. Firstly, Justine was with Elizabeth when the locket was taken. Then, of course, Justine didn't take the photographs of herself and Will. And, perhaps most importantly, what reason did Justine have to do all these terrible things?' said the head teacher.

whisper to speak very quietly

finally in the end

The head teacher continues speaking. 'But it isn't just Henry and Elizabeth who noticed you doing strange things. Another person saw you this morning – the bus driver. There are cameras on the bus, and the driver watched them this morning because he saw you put your hand into Justine's bag. He brought the film to the school and we watched it carefully. I could see you take Justine's phone and open the back of it.'

Vic stays silent. He feels bad about what he has done.

'They all hate me,' Vic thinks to himself. The bus driver, Henry... they have all made his plan go wrong. His parents look at him again and, finally, Vic starts to speak.

'I'm not a monster,' he says quietly. 'I'm unhappy. I'm always alone and I wanted a friend. The first day Will came to school he talked to me and he sat next to me, but then he left me. He went to play football and talk to Justine.'

'We're all listening,' says the head teacher.

'When I saw Justine with her group of friends I was angry and sad and I wanted revenge. I made another identity, #afriend, to make them feel as alone and unhappy as I feel. "They'll want me to be their friend if they're alone," I thought. But of course, I was wrong.'

'Open the window,' Vic's dad says, 'I feel faint.'

The head teacher quickly opens the window. 'Continue please,' he tells Vic.

'Justine invited everyone to her birthday party. She even invited Will – and he was just a new boy, but I was left out. Justine and her friends asked Will to go for coffee too, but they never asked me. I felt invisible and I wanted them to see me,' Vic whispers.

His mom looks up suddenly. 'But Vic, you did terrible things,' she says. 'I'm sorry you're sad because I want you to be happy. But you can't do nasty things to people. It's never right to be unkind.'

'I know that now, I feel terrible,' replies Vic. 'I saw Henry, Will, and Elizabeth this morning and I understood what a true friend is. You can't just make people like you, I can see that. I was wrong, I'm sorry, and I know I was unkind. When I saw you take Justine away I knew I had to tell the truth.'

The head teacher stops Vic. 'You're lucky, now Elizabeth has the locket back her parents don't want the police to do anything,' he explains. 'But the police still need to talk to you.'

Vic looks scared. Next, his dad asks the head teacher, 'If Vic says sorry to everyone can he come back to school?'

The head teacher shakes his head. 'No, Vic can't come to this school again,' he says slowly.

'But we can take his phone and computer away from him,' cries his mom. 'He can break his secret identity too. I know he's sorry that he was unkind.'

'I understand that,' says the head teacher. 'But he's done terrible things to people in his class. He really can't stay here. I think you need to move away and then Vic can have a new start. It's time for him to go to another school. It's for the best – he can make new friends and be happy there. He'll feel very strange at first, it's true. But when you're unkind, life isn't always easy, you see.'

'A new identity,' Vic thinks. 'A new school, a new start.'

Vic nods and his parents look surprised.

'I understand,' he tells the head teacher. 'I've learned an important lesson from all of this. I made a monster to make people unhappy; I scared people and didn't tell the truth. But I watched Henry, Elizabeth, and Will, and saw how kind they were to their friends. If I change school and start again, I'll meet new people and try to be a good friend, too.'

His mom smiles at Vic. 'Good work Vic, we'll help you all we can,' she says.

Vic imagines the monster walking away and leaving him. He does not feel trapped, he is free to start again and be happy. He stands up and walks to his parents and puts his arms around them. 'I'm sorry I worried you, and I'm sorry for what I've done,' he says. 'But I know this can be the start of better times.'

The head teacher is pleased. 'Vic, I need you to turn on your computer now and take the messages and photographs off the website,' he explains.

'Yes,' says Vic and he quickly does this.

'And now,' the head teacher continues, 'you must turn off #afriend, the identity you made.'

Vic tries to take the name off the website. He tries to stop the identity working but he cannot. 'Perhaps Henry can help,' he says. 'Henry is great at these things.'

Henry also tries, but #afriend is still there. 'It's OK,' says Henry. 'Nothing will happen until someone uses the identity. It can't do anything.'

Everyone agrees, it has finished and they can all forget what has happened. The monster has gone, trapped inside a website.

#afriend
log out
MENU
News
Messages
Friends
Games
Photos
ERROR:
unable to
delete profile

ACTIVITIES

READING CHECK

Match the characters with the events from the story.

1

2

3

4

5

6

a ...Vic's dad... is holding Vic's computer.

b .... sees Vic on the bus.

c .... tells the police about the memory card.

d .... are coming to talk to Vic.

e .... says Vic must leave the school.

f .... is very sad.

ACTIVITIES

WORD WORK

Match the words in the phone with the underlined words in the sentences.

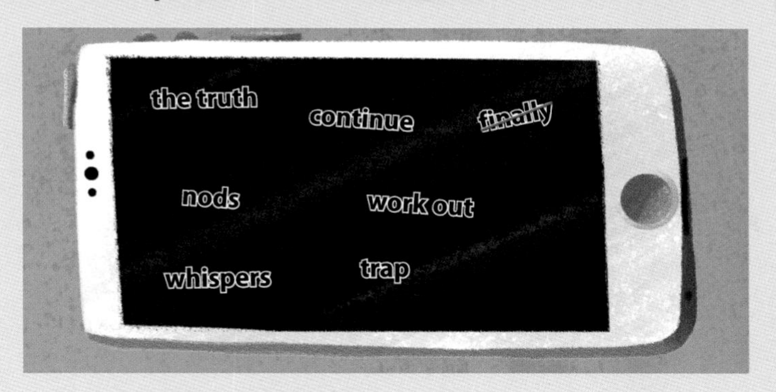

a At last, Vic answers the question. ....finally....

b Vic says he will not carry on writing messages. ....

c Henry speaks very quietly to Elizabeth. ....

d Vic stays silent but he moves his head up and down. ....

e 'It is time to tell us what really happened.' ....

f 'Henry can find the answer.' ....

g Vic thinks everyone wanted to use something to catch him. ....

GUESS WHAT

What happens after the story ends ? Answer the questions.

a How does Justine feel about Vic now she knows he was the monster?

....

b Vic says he understands how to be a friend. What do you think he has learned?

....

c What do you think happens to:

Henry and Elizabeth?

....

Will and Justine?

....

Project A Writing a story

1 Complete the first column of the table with information from *Who am I?*

	Who am I?	*Mary and Frankenstein*
Who is the main character?	Vic	Mary Shelley
What does the main character want?		
What does the main character do?		
What happens at the end?		

2 *Frankenstein* is a famous story. But who wrote it, and why? Read *Mary and Frankenstein*, then complete the second column of the table above.

Mary and Frankenstein

In 1816, three friends were on holiday in Switzerland, staying in a beautiful house by Lake Geneva. They were Lord Byron, Percy Shelley, and Mary Shelley, and they were all writers. It was a rainy day, and there was a terrible storm on the lake. The three friends were feeling bored. They wanted to do exciting things and have fun, and now they were trapped inside.

Later that day, after dinner, the friends sat around the fire, and listened to the wind and rain shaking the windows. 'I know,' said Lord Byron, 'We can each write a story and decide which one is the best. It must be a story that is dangerous and makes you want to scream. The winning story will make us afraid – we will not be able to sleep!' The other friends thought this was a good idea, and Lord Byron quickly wrote his story. Mary took a long time writing, but she was very pleased when she finished. In the end, her story was the best. The others sat by the fire and listened. Mary started to read, 'This is the story of Frankenstein,' she said, 'Victor Frankenstein and his terrible monster. '

3 You are going to write a story. First, complete the table with information about your story.

What is the title of your story?	
Who is the main character in the story?	
What does the main character want?	
What does the main character do?	
What happens at the end?	

4 Write your own story. Use the information from the table in Activity 3 and the phrases below to help you.

It was a cold/hot day…

She was… when…

He was feeling…

Later that day…

In the end…

Project B *Writing a diary*

1 Kate is a girl in Vic's class. Read her diary and complete the table.

Monday 15th

Monday morning, back to school. I don't like Mondays – I have very difficult lessons on Mondays, and also we have tennis in our sports lesson. I am not very good at playing tennis and it makes me angry running around after the tennis ball. And today Mr Waldman gave us a lot of homework to do – a very bad day. After school, I go and ride my horse – it is the best time of the day. It makes me happy feeding my horse and riding in the fields. Tomorrow is busy: I must go to the shops and buy a new dress for Justine's birthday party, and I need to buy her a present. I think I will ask some friends to come to the shops with me. Perhaps we can buy a pizza at the new café in town.

What day of the week is it?	Monday
Why was Kate feeling angry?	
What does Kate like doing?	
What must Kate do tomorrow?	

2 Use words and phrases from Activity 1 to fill in the blanks in Kate's diary.

Tuesday 16th

In the morning, we had a lesson with Mr Waldman. He wanted to see ..the homework.. we had to do last night. Luckily, I had finished all of it. Today was OK: in our sports lesson we played football and I enjoyed this much more than .... After school, I went .... with .... I wanted to buy .... for ...., and I had to buy .... for Justine. We were hungry, so we bought .... at .... I said goodbye to my friends because I had to go and see my .... Every day, I .... and .... my horse.

3 Use the sentences below to write about a day in the life of Kate.

In the evening, Kate went to ride her horse and feed him.
That afternoon, the teacher made the class stay late and Kate had to run for the bus.
Kate is learning something difficult in her English class today.
Kate was going shopping with her friends after school.

4 Choose one of the characters from the story and write a day from their diary.

GRAMMAR

GRAMMAR CHECK

Time clauses with *before*, *after*, *when*, and *while*

Before links a later action with an earlier action.

He needs a snack before he goes to sleep.

After links an earlier action with a later action.

After school, Vic looks for Henry because he needs help with his plan.

When links two actions close in time, often where the first action is the reason for the second action.

Usually she sings when she walks to the bus stop.

While is used for two actions happening at the same time, or for a background action that is going on when something else happens.

Justine is drinking a cola while she chats to Elizabeth.

We can put before, after, when, and while clauses at the end of the sentence.

Vic had a lot of things to get ready before he changed the memory cards.

1 Complete the sentences with *before*, *after*, *when*, or *while*.

a Vic is happy ....when..... he is talking to Will on the bus.

b Justine's parents said her party is going to finish .... 11 p.m. but .... midnight.

c Henry eats a snack .... he is working on his computer.

d Justine eats breakfast .... she walks to the bus stop every morning.

e The friends like to go to the café .... school and listen to music .... they eat fruit and drink coffee.

f Will goes to play football with the boys from the team .... someone kicks the ball to him.

g .... Vic writes the messages, he puts them on the website for everyone to read.

h Elizabeth is going to buy a new dress .... Justine's party.

GRAMMAR CHECK

Reflexive pronouns

We use reflexive pronouns (myself, yourself/yourselves, himself, herself, itself, ourselves, themselves) when the subject and the object of a verb are the same.

'Stop being stupid,' Vic tells himself.

We can also use reflexive pronouns to emphasize who did something, or for things that a person does alone without anybody else.

Justine wrote nothing herself.

I took the pictures myself.

2 Choose the correct reflexive pronoun from the computer screen to complete the sentences.

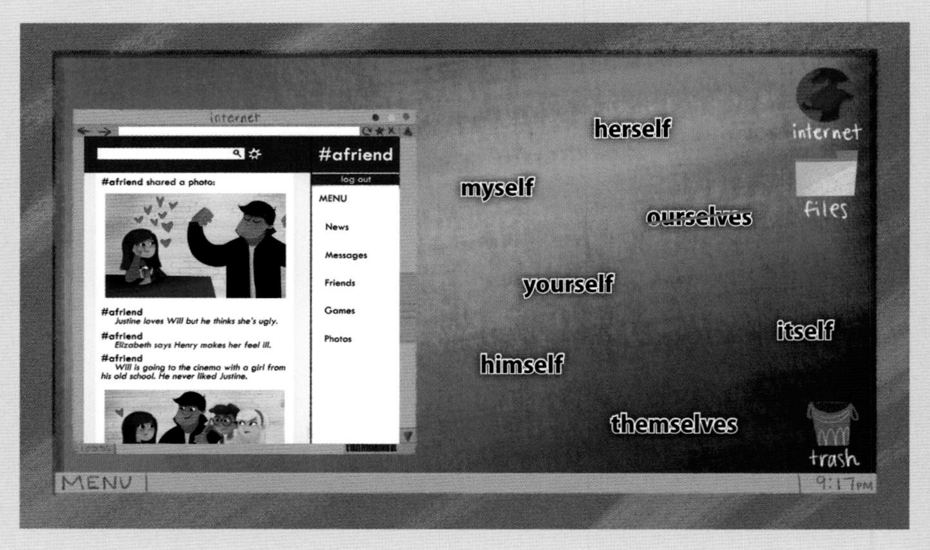

a 'We must take care of ..ourselves..,' said Justine to her friends.

b 'Why does he want a memory card ?' Henry was thinking to ....

c When the friends looked at the website, they saw the messages about ....

d 'The monster is going to make a mistake and show .... to us,' said the police.

e 'Are you ill? You do not look .... today,' Will said to Justine.

f Justine sang to .... on the way to school some mornings.

g 'I am going to find out who took my locket by ....,' Elizabeth told her parents.

GRAMMAR CHECK

Adjectives ending in *-y* and adverbs ending in *-ly*

We use adjectives to describe people or things. They go before nouns, or after verbs of appearance, like *be*, *seem*, and *look*. Some adjectives end in -y.

He makes Justine look ugly.

We often use adverbs to describe how something happens. Most adverbs of this type end in -ly.

'I don't play football,' says Vic quietly.

Some adjectives, such as *brotherly*, *fatherly*, *friendly*, and *motherly*, end in -ly, too.

3 Complete Justine's diary with the adjectives and adverbs below.

early	~~friendly~~	funny	happy	hungry	pretty	quickly	silly	sunny

DIARY

Today a new boy started school; he is called Will. He was talking to Vic on the bus; I think he was trying to be ...friendly... . I didn't say anything to him on the bus because I didn't want to look .... At lunch it was hot and ...., so we went outside. I watched while Will played football – he can run .... I think he was pleased when I asked him to the café: he looked .... He tells a lot of jokes and I think he is really .... We talked for a long time, and I think he was .... as he bought a pizza. Elizabeth was at the café with Henry; she looked so .... Tomorrow I am going to invite Will to my party, so I will arrive .... at the bus stop.

GRAMMAR

GRAMMAR CHECK

so*, *but*, and *because

We use so to talk about a result of something that happens.

Tell me about the people coming to the party so I know something about them.

We use because to talk about a reason why something happens.

Justine screamed because she was scared.

We use but to contrast two pieces of information.

They sit on the same bus every day, but Justine never speaks to him.

4 Match the first and second parts of these sentences.

a Vic stands outside the café,
b Justine is having a party
c The bus did not arrive on time,
d Henry takes his camera everywhere
e Will asked Justine a question,
f Vic changed the memory card
g Will likes playing sports,
h Vic's dad was late
i Justine likes fruit,
j Elizabeth is worried

1 but she did not answer.
2 so he plays football every day.
3 because he was busy at work.
4 because it is her birthday.
5 so everyone thought Justine was the monster.
6 because her mom is ill.
7 but not bananas.
8 so he can take pictures.
9 but he does not go in.
10 so everyone was late for school.

GRAMMAR CHECK

Indefinite pronouns and adverbs

We use indefinite pronouns ending in -body / -one and -thing instead of nouns to talk about people and things in a general way.

He wants to sit with someone and laugh.

We use singular verb forms with indefinite pronouns.

Everybody wants a friend.

We use indefinite adverbs ending in -where instead of a preposition.

She looked for the locket everywhere.

This table shows when to use which indefinite pronoun.

People	Things	Places
everyone / everybody	everything	everywhere
no one / nobody	nothing	nowhere
someone / somebody (+)	something (+)	somewhere (+)
anyone / anybody (- / ?)	anything (- / ?)	anywhere (- / ?)

5 Change the underlined words to the correct indefinite pronoun.

a Vic didn't want any person to see what he was doing.

..Vic didn't want anyone to see what he was doing..........

b Elizabeth looked in every place for her locket, but it wasn't there.

....

c Justine had done not one thing wrong; it was Vic who sent the message.

....

d Not one person knew that Vic was so unhappy at school.

....

e Henry was tired and didn't want to do a thing.

....

GRAMMAR CHECK

Participle phrases

In stories, we often talk about two actions that happen at the same time.

Mr Waldman leaves. He shuts the door noisily.

If the subject is the same for both verbs, it often sounds better to combine the sentences. We add a comma after the first verb phrase, then use the -ing form of the second verb.

Mr Waldman leaves, shutting the door noisily.

6 Use participle phrases to combine the pairs of sentences.

a Vic's mom was busy. She was cooking the dinner.

Vic's mom was busy, cooking the dinner.

b Vic lay in his room. He felt ill.

....

c Will is outside in the sun. He is running quickly.

....

d Elizabeth is alone. She is crying quietly.

....

e Justine was busy after school. She wrote invitations to her party.

....

GRAMMAR CHECK

Conditional sentences

We use if + present simple + will future to talk about the results of a possible situation.

If you take my locket, I'll cry.

We use if + present simple + imperative to tell or ask someone to do something in a possible situation.

If you want to meet my friends, come with me to the café.

The if clause can come at the start or the end of the sentence. When it comes at the start, we put a comma after it.

If you want a friend, be kind. *Be kind if you want a friend.*

7 Use the words in the box in the correct form to complete the sentences.

ask be buy ~~meet~~ play say

a If Vic starts a new school, ...he'll meet...... new friends.
b If the football team win, Will .... happy.
c If Will asks Justine to the cinema, ... yes.
d If Henry saves some money, ... a new computer.
e If her parents agree, Elizabeth .... Justine to stay at the weekend.
f If Will runs fast and kicks the ball, ... for the school football team.

8 Match the first and second parts of the sentences. Add a comma if it is needed.

a If he meets a friend — **3**
b Justine will be cross
c If he loses his camera
d If you come round after school
e If Will has new football boots
f Elizabeth will be happy
g Vic's mom worries

1 Henry will be angry.
2 we'll watch a film together.
3 Vic will be happy.
4 he'll wear them for the game tomorrow.
5 if her son is home late from school.
6 if Will is late for the cinema.
7 if her mom is better.

DOMINOES Your Choice

Read *Dominoes* for pleasure, or to develop language skills. It's your choice.

Each *Domino* reader includes:

- a good story to enjoy
- integrated activities to develop reading skills and increase vocabulary
- task-based projects – perfect for CEFR portfolios
- contextualized grammar activities

Each *Domino* pack contains a reader, and an excitingly dramatized audio recording of the story

If you liked this *Domino*, read these:

V is for Vampire

Lesley Thompson

'He's great, Vera,' said Angie.

When Viktor Sarav takes a job at Ballantine's, Angie and her brother Don – the young owners of the New York fashion company – are pleased. But soon there are strange deaths in the company. Is there a vampire at work at Ballantine's? Vera Donato, a company director with secrets to hide, is against Viktor. But Ed Valdemar, the company lawyer, trusts him. Who is right?

Virtual friends

Helen Salter

'You're in Paris and you aren't even happy to be here!' said Mum.

'So what?' I said. 'Places don't make you happy, do they? People make you happy. And all my friends are in London.'

Violet's mum moves to Paris, so she has to go too. Living in Paris as a fourteen year old girl should be very exciting, but Violet doesn't like it. Her only hope is to talk to her friends from London online. But will that work? Will Violet ever enjoy Paris? And what can she do about her Mum (who is so annoying…)?

	CEFR	Cambridge Exams	IELTS	TOEFL iBT	TOEIC
Level 3	B1	PET	4.0	57-86	550
Level 2	A2–B1	KET-PET	3.0-4.0	–	390
Level 1	A1–A2	YLE Flyers/KET	3.0	–	225
Starter & Quick Starter	A1	YLE Movers	1.0–2.0	–	–

You can find details and a full list of books and teachers' resources on our website:
www.oup.com/elt/gradedreaders